rrer

MAY 2023

Princess Truly
I Am Curious!

WRITTEN BY
Kelly Greenawalt

ART BY
Amariah Rauscher

ACORN™
SCHOLASTIC INC.

To Kaia—my curious, clever, and TRULY amazing
middle child. You are a glorious ray of sunshine! — KG

To Emma, Mikey, and Eli — AR

Text copyright © 2023 by Kelly Greenawalt
Illustrations copyright © 2023 by Amariah Rauscher

Library of Congress Cataloging-in-Publication Data

Names: Greenawalt, Kelly, author. | Rauscher, Amariah, illustrator.
Title: I am curious! / written by Kelly Greenawalt ; art by Amariah Rauscher.
Description: First edition. | New York : Acorn/Scholastic Inc., 2023. | Series: Princess Truly ; 7 |
Audience: Ages 4–6. | Audience: Grades K–1. | Summary: In rhyming text, Princess Truly visits the
science museum with her brother, solves the mystery of her missing snack, and uses her magic curls
to take a trip to outer space with her pup, Sir Noodles.
Identifiers: LCCN 2022011743 | ISBN 9781338818857 (paperback) | ISBN 9781338818864 (library binding)
Subjects: LCSH: Princesses—Juvenile fiction. | African American girls—Juvenile fiction. |
Curiosity—Juvenile fiction. | Brothers and sisters—Juvenile fiction. | Science museums—Juvenile fiction.|
Outer space—Juvenile fiction. | CYAC: Stories in rhyme. | Princesses—Fiction. |
African Americans—Fiction. | Curiosity—Fiction. | Brothers and sisters—Fiction. |
Science museums—Fiction. | Museums—Fiction. | Outer space—Fiction. |
BISAC: JUVENILE FICTION / Readers / Beginner | JUVENILE FICTION / Social Themes / Self-Esteem &
Self-Reliance | LCGFT: Stories in rhyme.
Classification: LCC PZ8.3.G7495 Iahg 2023 | DDC [E]—dc23
LC record available at https://lccn.loc.gov/2022011743

10 9 8 7 6 5 4 3 2 1   23 24 25 26 27

Printed in China   62

First edition, April 2023

Edited by Rachel Matson
Book design by Sarah Dvojack

Field Trip

I am Princess Truly.
I'm curious and smart.

I ask many questions.

I like big books and art.

I love to learn new things.
There is so much to see.

I want to take a trip.
My brother comes with me.

Look at that dinosaur!
This T. Rex is so tall.

The teeth look big and sharp.
Its arms are really small.

Next, we see butterflies.
Their wings are very neat.

They land on yummy fruit.
They taste it with their feet.

Look at the giant tank!
Ty really likes the shark.

We watch the jellies swim.
They glow blue in the dark.

It's time for the movie.
We see a spotted seal.

We watch a dolphin swim.

We learn about an eel.

Now the movie is done.
We wave to the stingray.

This trip was so much fun.
We learned a lot today!

The Missing Snack

It's time for movie night!
I made a yummy snack.

I go get my blanket,

and then I come right back.

Where did my popcorn go?
How did it disappear?

I think someone took it.
I'm sure I left it here.

I am a detective.
I know just what to do.

I can find my popcorn.
I must look for a clue.

Aha! I see popcorn.
It's right there on the floor.

I follow the long trail.
It leads right to a door.

I open up the door.
I spot another clue.

Someone made a big mess.
They spilled the syrup, too.

There are sticky footprints.
I see milk on the floor.

I follow the footprints.
The mess stops at Ty's door.

I go into Ty's room.
My brother swiped my snack!

I solved the mystery.
I have my popcorn back.

Blast Off!

I look up at the moon.
I gaze at all the stars.

I want to go to space.
I want to fly by Mars.

Sir Noodles wants to come.
I know just what to do.

We need rainbow magic.
We need a spaceship, too.

I shake my magic curls.
They glimmer and they glow.

3, 2, 1, we blast off!
Out into space we go.

We pass the Big Dipper.
The stars are shining bright.

Look! There is a comet.
It makes a pretty light.

We pass by the planets.
We are learning new things.

Mars is smaller than Earth,
and Saturn has eight rings.

Next, we land on the moon.
We put on our space suits.

There is so much to see.
We use our rocket boots.

Exploring has been fun.

We need to go home soon.

We hop in our spaceship.
We wave bye to the moon.

About the Creators

Kelly Greenawalt lives just outside of Houston, Texas. She is the mom of seven curious kids who love to learn and visit new places. Princess Truly was inspired by her daughters, Calista and Kaia, who have magical curls and big imaginations.

Amariah Rauscher has always been a curious person. She loves to go to museums, especially the ones with dinosaurs and lots of creepy crawly bugs. Amariah lives with her family in the New Orleans area. When she isn't at a museum, she can be found drawing, painting, or reading a good book.

Read these books featuring Princess Truly!

YOU CAN DRAW A SPACESHIP!

1 Draw a cone shape.

2 Draw the spaceship's body. Add two circles. Those are windows!

3 Add the spaceship's center fin. Draw two short lines to connect it to the sides of the ship.

4 Draw two more fins— one on each side of the ship's body.

5 Add a door to the spaceship.

6 Color in your drawing!

WHAT'S YOUR STORY?

Princess Truly explores outer space.
Imagine that **you** are going to space!
How would you get there?
What would you see?
Write and draw your story!